Spies to the Rescue . . .

A tunnel lay before Cassie and Zeke. The smell of animals was stronger than ever.

The two spies followed it, around a corner and down one tunnel after another. When finally the last tunnel spilled out into a room, Cassie felt sickened by what she saw. The walls were lined with cages, stacked one on top of the other. And inside the cages were the missing animals.

Look for the other exciting books in the series
The Spy from Outer Space:

Alien Alert!

Too Many Spies

Escape from Earth

Available now!

HES.

4

SPIES, INCORPORATED

Debra Hess

Illustrated by Carol Newsom

Hyperion Paperbacks for Children
New York

Produced by Chardiet Unlimited, Inc., 33 West 17th Street,
New York, New York 10011.

A Hyperion Paperback original

First edition: March 1994

1 3 5 7 9 10 8 6 4 2

Library of Congress Cataloging-in-Publication Data

Hess, Debra
Spies, Incorporated/Debra Hess; illustrated by Carol Newsom—1st ed.
    p.   cm.—(The spy from outer space; #4)
Summary: When Hillsdale's pets begin to disappear, it is up to ten-year-
old Cassie, her classmate Ben, and Zeke, a boy from outer space, to
figure out what is happening to them.
ISBN 1-56282-683-2 (pbk.)
[1. Extraterrestrial beings—Fiction. 2. Science Fiction. 3. Mystery and
detective stories.]
I. Newsom, Carol, ill.   II. Title.   III. Series: Hess, Debra. Spy from
outer space; #4.
PZ7.H4326Sp   1994
[Fic]—dc20   93-34116
                    CIP
                    AC

For Alexa, with love

SPIES, INCORPORATED

CHAPTER

Cassie Williams, president and founder of Spies, Incorporated, burst through the garage door and stomped the mud off her boots. In all her ten years on Earth, this was the rainiest, muddiest spring vacation she could remember.

"What a waste of time!" she exclaimed.

"Couldn't find him?" asked Ben O'Brien, glancing up from the comic book he was reading.

"He wasn't missing!" said Cassie. "He was hiding. That stupid baby-sitter didn't even realize they were playing hide-and-seek. Any other cases come in while we were out?"

"You're kidding, right?" said Ben.

"Very funny!" said Cassie, slipping out of her yellow slicker and letting it fall into a puddle on the floor. She flopped into a chair and groaned. She was beginning to think that opening a spy shop had not been her brightest idea after all. She had thought it would be a fun way to actually get paid for spying during spring break. But Spies, Incorporated had been open since the day after school had closed, and so far the baby-sitter had been their first—and only—client.

"Where's Zeke?" asked Ben.

Cassie pointed out the window. Zeke was racing around the yard, his head tilted toward the sky and his mouth open, trying to catch raindrops.

"He's like some little kid," said Ben.

Cassie laughed. "I know," she said. "It's hard to believe it doesn't rain on Triminica."

"Doesn't rain *water*," Ben corrected her. Then he yawned and stretched his arms over his head.

"I'm bored," he whined.

Cassie sighed. She didn't want to admit it, but she was bored, too. Everything seemed boring since she had traveled to outer space. What could compare with flying in spaceships and escaping evil aliens?

Cassie glanced over at Ben, who had his head buried back in his comic book. It was hard to believe that she and the class bully had shared such an amazing adventure—and even harder to believe how that adventure had changed Ben. But then, ever since Zeke had come into her life, Cassie had learned to expect the unexpected.

Zeke, whose real name Cassie could not pronounce, was an alien from the planet Triminica.

Early that fall, he and his family had accidentally landed their spaceship on Earth. For Cassie, a would-be spy with no one to spy with, it was a dream come true. Zeke was a student at the Interstellar Spy Academy. He was also exactly Cassie's age. The two had become best friends almost instantly.

But the day finally came when Zeke had to return to his planet. Unfortunately, it was the same day Ben O'Brien figured out Zeke was an alien and sneaked on board the spaceship. Before anyone could stop the chain of events, Cassie and Ben were hurtling through space with the Triminicans—only to find the ship was under enemy command. They had landed on a dangerous transport station on the edge of Zeke's galaxy. Once there, the two Earthlings had only narrowly escaped the evil Delphs, an owllike race of creatures who hated the Triminicans and wanted to experiment on human children.

Cassie shivered just thinking about the Delphs. They had been hiding right in Hillsdale, and no one ever suspected it! Of course, no one ever went near the abandoned house at the end of Whisper Wind Lane. Everyone said it was haunted. What would the people of Hillsdale have done if they had discovered that the house *was* inhabited, not by ghosts, but by aliens living in secret tunnels beneath the house? Cassie almost laughed out loud at the thought.

She could laugh because everything had turned out all right—actually, better than all right, because Zeke was back in Hillsdale for six months while his parents went in search of other Triminicans stranded on Earth.

But now Ben O'Brien knew Zeke's secret identity. And while it seemed that the boy who had been a bully since kindergarten had really changed in outer space, Cassie had learned never to trust the obvious. So when Ben had insisted on joining Spies, Incorporated in exchange for keeping his mouth shut, Cassie and Zeke had agreed.

Just then Ben threw his comic book down on the desk, groaned, and stood up.

"Let's *do* something!" he said.

As if in answer, the door swung open, and Zeke tromped in happily. He was soaking wet.

"I believe I was able to catch more than twenty raindrops in my mouth!" he announced proudly.

Cassie and Ben looked at each other and laughed.

"That is not impressive?" asked Zeke.

"Oh, it's very impressive," said Cassie, bringing Zeke a towel so he could dry off. "It's just that we've never seen anyone who liked rain as much as you do."

"No one older than five," Ben scoffed.

"Ben!" said Cassie. "Just because you're bored is no reason to be mean to Zeke."

"Sorry," Ben grumbled. He sipped at his grape soda and turned to look out the window.

"Hey," he said suddenly. "Snob alert!"

Cassie looked out. Marilee Tischler was standing by the garage door in her matching raincoat and umbrella. Cassie groaned. She always groaned when she saw Marilee Tischler. Marilee was the prettiest, richest, snottiest girl in Cassie's class, and Cassie couldn't stand her.

Marilee knocked.

Reluctantly Cassie rolled open the garage door but then stood directly in front of it, not letting Marilee inside.

"Hi, Cassie!" said Marilee, smiling her usual snaky smile.

"Marilee," said Cassie, not smiling at all.

"May I come in?" asked Marilee.

"What do you want?" asked Cassie.

"I want to hire you—you spies," Marilee announced.

"Yeah?" asked Cassie. "To do what?"

"My cat is missing!"

"So call the fire department," said Cassie.

"You don't understand," whined Marilee. "The maid was taking care of the cat while my family was down in the Caribbean. Cassie, are you going to let me come inside or not?"

"I guess so," said Cassie, finally moving back

so Marilee could enter. Marilee collapsed her umbrella in her usual dainty fashion and stepped inside the garage. As soon as she saw Zeke, her whole face lit up like a Christmas tree.

"Hi, Zeke. Do you like my tan?" she asked, batting her eyes flirtatiously.

"The cat!" Cassie snapped. "Get back to the cat!"

"Well," Marilee huffed. "As I said, the maid was taking care of my cat while I was on vacation. And one day, she just wasn't there."

"The maid?" asked Ben. Cassie stifled a laugh.

"No, stupid. The cat!" snapped Marilee.

"Don't call me stupid!" Ben yelled.

"Maybe she had a date with a male cat," said Cassie.

"Impossible!" said Marilee. "She simply isn't allowed out of the house."

Poor cat, thought Cassie.

"Are you going to find her or not?" asked Marilee.

"Yeah, I guess so," said Cassie. "Ben, you stay here and write up any other cases. Zeke and I will return to the scene of the crime." Ben looked annoyed but grumbled yeah and settled back into his comic book.

Cassie and Zeke followed Marilee home. The two spies combed every inch of the Tischlers' huge house, picking up bits of cat hair here and there, examining an unraveled ball of string, peering at the uneaten dish of cat food. They even interviewed the maid. After sleuthing for an hour, the spies had to admit that the cat was gone. But they also had to admit that they had absolutely no idea *where*.

"Sorry, Marilee," said Cassie as she headed for the front door.

"That's it?" cried Marilee.

"What else do you expect us to do?" asked Zeke.

"I expect you to find my cat!"

"Maybe she'll come home on her own," said Cassie

"Some spies you are!" Marilee huffed, sniffling back a tear.

Suddenly Cassie felt sorry for Marilee. "Maybe your father will buy you a new cat," she said.

It was the wrong thing to say.

"I don't want a new cat!" wailed Marilee. "I want Fluffy!"

"Fluffy?" Zeke mouthed at Cassie.

Cassie and Zeke left Marilee in the doorway to her house and returned to the headquarters of Spies, Incorporated. Cassie was silent as they walked along. She was torn between feeling sorry for Marilee and being secretly pleased that something had finally upset the girl who had been so mean so many times. As they walked up the driveway to her house, Cassie

8

turned to ask Zeke if he thought her feelings were normal.

But just then Cassie heard a huge commotion coming from inside the garage. She and Zeke took one look at each other and then broke into a run. When they opened the garage door they could hardly believe their eyes. Ben O'Brien was surrounded by a dozen frantic, screaming children.

Cassie and Zeke stood in the entrance to the garage, trying to make sense of the craziness inside. There were kids of all ages and sizes, all bundled in rain slickers, all flailing their arms and screaming at once.

"Can you hear what they're yelling about?" Cassie leaned over and said loudly into Zeke's ear.

"Animals!" he called back above the din.

Cassie tried to focus on the words. Bit by bit she was able to pick up snippets of sentences.

"My dog . . . !"

" . . . stole my ferret!"

" . . . lizard . . ."

Finally, Cassie couldn't stand it anymore. She brought two fingers to her lips and whistled. The room was suddenly silent. And then, just as suddenly, the noise started up again. Only this time everyone was screaming at Cassie.

As near as the young spy could tell, the animals had started disappearing two days ago. Children returning from vacation, or a weekend at Grandma's, or a trip to the mall all discovered that their cherished pets were missing. One kid had even managed to lose a goldfish—bowl and all.

"We need to get organized," Zeke mouthed at Cassie as they listened to a little girl crying about a lost parakeet.

Cassie nodded, leaped to the top of the table, and held up her hands.

"Anyone who keeps talking will have to leave immediately!" she shrieked over the noise.

Slowly the roar of voices settled down.

"Okay!" said Cassie. "This is what we're going to do: Everyone line up. Then one by one tell me, Zeke, or Ben exactly what happened. We will write down the information and your phone numbers. Then we will call and tell you if we will take your case or not."

The noise started up again almost immediately, and it took more than an hour for the three spies to get all the information. But finally the garage was peaceful once again, and Spies, Incorporated held its first real meeting.

"I think we should take Marilee's case and the case of the missing goldfish!" said Ben, slurping from a mug of steaming hot chocolate that Cassie's mom had brought in.

"Why?" asked Cassie, blowing on her own cocoa.

"They said they would pay the most money!" Ben exclaimed as if it were obvious.

"Maybe so," said Zeke thoughtfully. "But we found no leads at all at Marilee's house. . . ."

"And how do you find a missing goldfish?" Cassie finished for him.

"Let us hear the cases out loud," said Zeke.

Cassie took another sip of cocoa and consulted the stack of papers in front of her. Ben had written down *every* word each kid had said, and there was something sticky on his pages that smelled suspiciously like grape soda. Zeke had his information in some strange order, and Cassie had scrawled hers so quickly she could barely read her own handwriting. After squinting at the pages for a minute, she went inside the house. She returned with one of her father's long yellow pads of paper. Then she went to work making a single list.

Person	*Missing Pet*
Marilee Tischler	Cat (female)
Karen Slopes	Lizard
Matt Clark	Bowl of goldfish
Sara Henderson	2 dogs (golden retriever and terrier)
Tyrell Hughes	Boa constrictor
Amanda Carson	Ferret

Stacy and Stan Swarthope	2 gerbils
Bobby Barsky	Bugs
Kendra Jones	Cat (male)
Cynthia Kim	Turtle
Michael Malone	Rabbit
Kayla Tyson	Parakeet

Cassie read the list out loud.

"Wow!" cried Ben. "Tyrell Hughes has a boa constrictor? I can't believe it. He's such a puny little kid."

Cassie rolled her eyes at Zeke. "He isn't puny, Ben," she said. "He's only seven years old."

"What is a boa constrictor?" asked Zeke.

"It's a very dangerous snake," said Cassie.

"And you feed it live things like mice and chickens," added Ben, his eyes gleaming.

"That is disgusting!" said Zeke.

"No it isn't!" said Ben. "It's totally cool. I can't believe some little seven year old's parents let him have such a great pet."

Cassie sighed and looked back at one of her own scrawled sheets.

"You'll be happy to know it's really Tyrell's older brother's snake. Tyrell was the one who knew about our spy shop, so he was the one who came over here."

"Let's look for the boa!" Ben said eagerly.

"Ben, you're completely missing the point of this!" Cassie exclaimed.

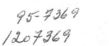

"Oh yeah?" said Ben. "What *is* the point?"

"The point is that suddenly all these animals are missing, which is very, very strange!"

Ben was silent. "Hey, yeah—you're right!" he said suddenly.

"Who would want to take all these animals?" asked Zeke.

"That is a very good question!" said Cassie.

Zeke leaned over and took the long list from Cassie. He studied it for a moment.

"I am not certain what a ferret or a rabbit is," he said finally. "But I do find it quite strange that the only animal mentioned more than once is the cat. And even then, it appears to be one female cat and one male cat!"

"Yeah, you're right!" cried Cassie. "That *is* weird."

"Kind of like someone's starting an animal collection," Ben muttered.

Cassie looked at Ben in surprise. It always startled her when Ben said something smart. She was never quite sure if he was a dumb kid who was smart occasionally or a smart kid who had gotten used to behaving as though he were dumb.

"I think you're right, Ben!" she said. "But who?"

"And where do we begin looking?" asked Zeke.

"Cassie!" called Mrs. Williams from inside the house. "It's time to go!"

14

Cassie groaned. This was her least favorite part of spring break.

"Where are you going?" asked Zeke.

"Carson's department store has this huge sale every year at this time," Cassie grumbled as she stood up and started tidying the stack of papers.

"School resumes tomorrow, correct?" asked Zeke.

"Correct," said Cassie sadly.

"Then I will return to the ship now and see you in the morning. Perhaps we can begin working on these cases tomorrow afternoon."

"Hey—maybe Spot can help us!" Cassie suggested.

Spot was Zeke's robot. He had been left in charge while Mirac and Inora, Zeke's parents, were searching the planet for other Triminicans. Zeke and Spot lived on a spaceship that was parked in a field at the edge of town. When the invisibility shield was activated, no one could see the ship.

"CASSIE!" Mrs. Williams was getting impatient.

"I've got to go!" said Cassie. "See you tomorrow!"

After what seemed like hours of trying on sweaters and jeans, Cassie's shopping ordeal was finally over. All through it and dinner with her family, Cassie's mind was on the missing pets. But it wasn't until that night, when she was finishing a snack of milk and cookies at the kitchen table, that her eyes fell on the evening edition of the *Hillsdale News.* The headline made her gasp.

POLAR BEAR MISSING FROM LOCAL ZOO!

CHAPTER 3

Cassie, Ben, and the Spy from Outer Space arrived early at school the next day—only to find that the animals were missing from there, too. All the fish, all the turtles, every single animal that had been left at Hillsdale Elementary over the spring break was missing. All day long, students raced up to Cassie or Ben or Zeke and begged them to find their missing animals. Even one of the teachers asked if perhaps Cassie wanted to try to find the white mice missing from the science room. By the end of the day the spies were more confused than ever. They agreed to go to Zeke's spaceship to talk.

After the final bell rang, the three of them met at the far end of the playground. Cassie scanned the area to see if anyone was watching.

"All clear!" she announced.

"Ben, take Cassie's hand!" Zeke ordered.

"No way!" said Ben.

"Fine, stay behind then," said Zeke as he

punched coordinates into the golden disk and then took Cassie's hand.

"I thought you wanted to travel by materializer," Cassie said to Ben.

"I do," said Ben.

"Then don't be a jerk," said Cassie. "I have a feeling Zeke would be perfectly happy leaving you here."

Zeke threw the golden pancakelike disk. It arced high and wide in the still cloudy sky and then boomeranged back at the cluster of spies.

Ben reached out and grabbed Cassie's hand.

The disk raced toward them at a ferocious speed. But just when it looked as if it would hit Cassie smack in the stomach, the materializer veered out and began circling the spies, trailing a cloud of sparkling light behind it. Faster and faster the disk spun, the circles of light spinning and twinkling. As Cassie felt her feet leave the ground, she heard Ben cry out.

"WOW!"

A moment later the three spies crashed down in the control room of the spaceship.

"Greetings!" intoned a mechanical voice.

Cassie looked up from where she sat on the floor and grinned into the large, hollow eyes of the Triminicans' robot.

"Hi, Spot!" she said.

"I see your landings are still problematic," said Spot.

19

"Very funny." Cassie laughed in spite of herself.

"That was great!" cried Ben.

"Why did you bring him?" asked Spot, pointing an accordioned arm at Ben.

In the short time the Triminicans had been on Earth, the robot had grown fond of Cassie— at least as fond as a robot could be of a human. After all, it was Cassie who had come up with the name Spot—*and* the dog disguise that kept the robot from being discovered while on an alien planet.

Spot's feelings—simulated feelings—about Ben were quite different, however. Ben was responsible for all the trouble they had had in outer space. And now he was responsible for Spot and the Triminicans' being back on Earth.

"Hiya, Spot!" said the ex-bully cheerfully.

The robot ignored him. Ben shrugged and went to stare at the cylindrical tube of bubbling, spitting pink liquid that stood in the center of the control room.

"Let us go into the sitting room," said Zeke.

The three spies settled themselves on the floating cushions of light that served as chairs. Spot remained standing.

"Robot, we need your help," said Zeke. "A polar bear is missing from the zoo!"

"And Tyrell Hughes's boa constrictor is gone!" Ben chimed in.

"And the animals from school . . . ," Cassie added.

"All gone!" said Ben.

"And we could not find Marilee's cat," cried Zeke.

"No one knows what's going on," said Cassie.

"Except for whoever is responsible," Zeke reminded her. Cassie nodded and looked at Spot.

"We need to figure out what all this means!" she said. "I don't suppose you have any ideas?"

Spot was silent for a moment. Cassie thought she could hear the computer whirring in his brain.

"It seems obvious," he finally droned.

"Oh, really?" said Cassie, rolling her eyes at Zeke.

Zeke grinned. "Okay, Robot. What is so obvious?"

"Have you asked the question, Why are these animals missing?"

"Of course we've asked that!" exclaimed Ben. "We just haven't answered it yet."

"It seems logical that someone or some group of individuals is collecting these animals as specimens," Spot stated.

"So?" said Ben.

"So, it would then logically follow that they will not stop until they have collected all the specimens they possibly can," said Spot.

"And?" Cassie urged him on.

"Set a trap, of course," said Spot.

"Of course!" said Zeke.

21

"Of course what?" asked Ben.

"We lure the thieves to us with an animal they don't have yet and then follow them back to their hideout. Is that what you mean, Spot?" asked Cassie.

"Affirmative."

"That's great!" said Cassie. "That way we can find out who's stealing the animals and recover them at the same time! Only—what kind of animal should we use as bait?"

"Something rare!" said Zeke.

"Something big so they can't miss it!" said Ben.

"Where are we going to get a big, rare animal?" asked Cassie.

The spies were silent for a moment. And then, suddenly, as if they shared one brain, all three heads swiveled toward Spot.

"NO!" said Spot.

"Oh, come on, Spot," said Cassie. "You're already used to your Earth dog disguise. We'll just make you something rarer and larger this time."

"NO!" said Spot.

"How about a lion?" Ben suggested.

"NO!" shouted the robot.

"I have to agree with Spot," said Cassie. "Lions are too dangerous. If someone else saw him, they would call the zoo."

"A kangaroo!" Ben announced triumphantly as if it were the greatest idea he had ever had.

Cassie shook her head. "We would have too much trouble making Spot look like a kangaroo."

"Well, what about a gorilla!" said Ben.

"GORILLA?!" said Spot.

"Don't worry, Spot," Cassie said gently, shooting Ben a fierce look. "We won't make you be anything in the ape family."

"Why not?" asked Ben.

"We just won't, okay?" said Cassie. She didn't feel like trying to explain how Spot had once been captured by zoo officials and how, when he tried to escape, he had ended up in a cage full of gorillas and . . . well, all in all, it had been a horrible experience for the poor robot.

Cassie studied Spot again, trying to figure out exactly which animal she could make him look like.

"What about a dinosaur?" said Ben.

"A what?" asked Zeke.

"The dinosaur is an extinct Earth creature . . . ," Spot began to report, but Cassie cut him off.

"I've got it!" she cried. "A penguin!"

"A what?" asked Zeke again.

"A penguin?" said Ben.

"A PENGUIN?" shrieked Spot. "You want me to simulate a bird?"

"It would be a really easy costume to make," said Cassie. "Much easier than gluing all those wigs on you to make you look like a dog. All we have to do is get a barrel, paint it black and white, slip you into it, paint your face . . . "

"Don't forget to give him a beak," Ben added.

"Oh yeah," said Cassie. "And a beak. And then you'll look like a penguin. And the best part is, we won't have to teach you how to waddle 'cause it will be the only way you can walk in the barrel!"

"Penguins are not indigenous to this part of your country," Spot protested.

"Huh?" said Ben.

"He means that penguins don't live in Hillsdale," Cassie explained. Then she looked at the robot and grinned.

"But you're wrong, Spot," she said. "There are penguins at the Hillsdale Zoo. And maybe the thieves will think one escaped!"

"The zoo?" said Spot desperately.

"Don't worry, Spot," said Cassie. "I promise we won't let them take you to the zoo again."

"Zekephlon, you will not let them do this, will you?" pleaded Spot, sounding almost human.

Zeke grinned. "Yes, I will, Robot. But we will attach a tracking device to you. And we will rescue you no matter where they take you!"

Spot seemed to contemplate this for a minute. "May I program this tracking device to feed coordinates to the ship's computer in the event you are unable to actually follow me?" he asked.

"An excellent idea!" said Zeke. "Perhaps you

could also program the computer to automatically feed those same coordinates to a materializer disk I will carry with me at all times."

"And maybe that disk could sound an alarm of some sort," said Ben eagerly.

"Yeah," said Cassie. "That way no matter when Spot is nabbed, we'll know!"

And that is how there came to be a very strange-looking penguin waddling up and down the streets of Hillsdale the next day.

CHAPTER 4

The next afternoon Cassie was doodling penguins piloting spaceships in her notebook when she heard a series of high-pitched beeps coming from across the room. She glanced over at Zeke, who fumbled in his pocket for a second, then looked up at her and grinned.

"What was that noise?" barked Ms. Marston, their math teacher, from where she stood at the blackboard.

No one in the class said anything.

Zeke raised his hand.

"Yes, Zeke?" said Ms. Marston impatiently.

"May I be excused please?"

"Does this have anything to do with that sound?" asked the teacher.

"What sound?" asked Zeke.

Cassie stifled a giggle.

Luckily the bell signaling the end of school rang at that moment. Cassie sprang from her seat and ran to Zeke's side.

"Was that Spot?" she asked.

Zeke nodded. "Let's go!"

The two spies ran outside to the playground. The blacktop was covered with puddles of water, but for the first time in weeks, it hadn't rained all day. Cassie leaned against the damp brick wall where dodgeball was played during drier weather.

"Well?" she said.

"He is still moving," said Zeke, consulting the small device in his hands. "When he stops, we will materialize to the coordinates."

"I've been thinking about that, Zeke," said Cassie. "The kidnappers—whoever they are—might still be there. We should probably wait a while before just materializing at some unknown place."

"You are right," said Zeke. "And perhaps we should appear a short distance from the coordinates also."

"Or . . . ," said Cassie thoughtfully, "we could go back to your ship and use the computer to find out exactly where the coordinates are before we go anywhere!"

"Cassie!" Zeke exclaimed. "I am impressed. I did not realize you had such an understanding of the capacity of our computer." Cassie smiled at the compliment.

"Thanks," she said. "I hate to disappoint you, but I remembered the computer could do stuff like this from the time we rescued Spot from the zoo."

The two spies had materialized on board the ship and gulped down a quick sandwich before they remembered that Ben was now part of their spy team, too.

"Should we go back and get him?" Cassie asked halfheartedly.

"No," said Zeke.

"We'll just tell him it happened so quickly we didn't have time to get to his classroom and get him," said Cassie.

"Sure," said Zeke, focused on the device in his hand. "Hey—Spot has stopped moving!"

"Really?" said Cassie, excited.

They waited five minutes to make sure Spot wasn't going to move again. Then Zeke moved to the main control panel of the ship's computer, pulled up a map of Hillsdale, and punched in the coordinates. A moment later a light flashed on the map.

"That is odd," he said.

He repeated the procedure. The light flashed in exactly the same place.

"Cassie—look!" Zeke exclaimed.

Cassie peered at the map, and a shiver ran up her spine. "I don't believe it," she gasped.

The light was flashing on the house at the end of Whisper Wind Lane—the very same abandoned house where Cassie and Zeke had found the evil Delphs hiding out, though of course they hadn't known they were Delphs at the time.

"This is one strange coincidence," said Zeke.

"It is a coincidence, isn't it?" Cassie asked softly.

"Of course it is," said Zeke. "This is probably the only empty house in all of Hillsdale. It is the logical place for the kidnappers to have chosen."

"I'm sure that's it!" said Cassie. But she wasn't sure at all. What if the Delphs had returned to Earth?

"They would not have followed us here," said Zeke, as though reading Cassie's thoughts. "There is nothing for them on this planet."

"I know," said Cassie. "I just can't believe that after all these years of that house being completely empty . . . " She didn't finish her thought. She didn't have to. Zeke knew exactly what she was thinking.

"It is simply a very strange coincidence," he repeated.

The two spies put on their spy belts and materialized outside the house at the end of Whisper Wind Lane. Then they hid behind a tree to take watch. There were no lights on, no sounds, no sign of anyone inside. Cassie slipped around to the back of the house and peered in the basement window where she had once seen a mysterious alien meeting. All was dark and silent. She returned to Zeke's side.

After ten minutes Zeke activated the tracking device again. Spot's signal came in louder than ever. It was definitely coming from inside the house.

"Let us go in!" said Zeke.

Cassie agreed. But just as they were about to step out from behind the tree, she grabbed her friend's arm and whispered harshly.

"ZEKE!"

Zeke looked up and froze. Two men were coming out of the house, their heads together, deep in conversation. Cassie and the Spy from Outer Space watched from behind the tree as the men walked to a van parked halfway down the street, got in, and quickly drove off.

"Did you see their faces?" Cassie asked breathlessly.

Zeke shook his head.

"Not clearly. Did you?"

"No," said Cassie. "They were too far away and too huddled together. If only they weren't driving we could have followed them."

"We are here to rescue Spot," Zeke reminded her. "And perhaps locate the other animals."

"Right!" Cassie agreed. "Let's go. And let's hope there's no one else inside."

With a blast of zorcanian 6, a Triminican metal dissolver, Zeke melted the lock on the front door of the house, and the two spies

30

slipped inside. Zeke immediately sniffed the air.

"Do you smell something?" he asked Cassie.

Cassie inhaled deeply and then coughed. "Yuck!" she said.

"What is it?" asked Zeke.

"It smells like the zoo!" Cassie exclaimed.

"ANIMALS!" they both cried at the same time.

Zeke consulted the device in his hand once again. It started beeping so loudly, Cassie covered her ears with her hands.

"Turn it off!" she shouted over the noise.

Zeke flipped a switch, and the sound died out. Slowly he pointed at a door. Cassie gulped. They had been through this door once before. It led to the basement—and to the tunnels where they now knew the Delphs had once hidden.

"Spot is down there!" announced Zeke.

"Let's go!" said Cassie, trying to sound braver than she felt.

The spies raced down the basement stairs. Cassie went immediately to the wall.

"The tunnels must be here somewhere," she said, running her hands along the wall. But she couldn't find an opening anywhere.

"Try knocking," Zeke suggested.

"What? Why?"

"It will show us where the wall is thinnest," said Zeke. "Maybe that way we can find the entrance."

Cassie and Zeke tapped along the wall. Finally,

31

Cassie found a spot where the sound echoed back hollowly. She stopped and removed a flashlight from her spy belt. A ridge ran vertically along the wall.

"I think this is it!" she called to Zeke. "How do we get in?"

"Maybe there is a switch," said Zeke.

Cassie looked everywhere for a switch or button that would open the wall, but she found nothing.

"Maybe we should blast it open!" she suggested.

"With what?" asked Zeke.

Cassie shrugged. She was out of ideas. She leaned heavily against the wall in frustration— and fell back as the wall gave way behind her.

"Cassie, you did it!" cried Zeke.

Sure enough a stream of light now flooded the room from an opening in the wall. A tunnel lay before Cassie and Zeke. The smell of animals was stronger than ever.

The two spies followed it, around a corner and down one tunnel after another. When finally the last tunnel spilled out into a room, Cassie felt sickened by what she saw. The walls were lined with cages, stacked one on top of the other. And inside the cages were the missing animals.

"Zekephlon," clicked a mechanical voice.

"Robot!" Zeke ran to the cage holding the odd-looking penguin. He quickly melted the lock and freed his friend.

"What should we do with these other animals?" Zeke asked once that was completed. But Cassie had moved to the far end of the room, where she stood, mouth open, hardly breathing, staring at the scariest list she had ever read.

AARDVARK	male		female	✓
ANT	male	✓	female	
ANTEATER	male		female	
ANTELOPE	male		female	✓
BAT	male		female	
BEAR (BROWN)	male		female	
BEAR (POLAR)	male	✓	female	
BIRDS (ALL SPECIES)	male		female	
CAT	male	✓	female	✓

The list went on and on, listing every Earth animal Cassie had ever heard of. But the thing that scared Cassie most were the little check marks next to the animals that had already been collected. She felt like she was looking at a list that Noah would have made for the ark—a list of all the creatures to be collected before the rest of life on Earth was destroyed!

CHAPTER

5

Zeke and the penguin joined Cassie by the wall.

"What is it?" asked Zeke, staring at the list.

"Some really sick person is collecting all the animals in the universe or something," said Cassie.

"All the animals on planet Earth," the penguin corrected her.

Cassie shivered and looked away. The room they were in was dark and dank and smelled of the many animals. And it was barely big enough to accommodate all the cages. There were so many creatures! Every animal from Spies, Incorporated's list of missing pets, plus many more.

Just then a low growl from a corner of the room made Cassie start. Peering into the darkness, she saw the enormous shape of a polar bear.

"What are we going to do with all these animals?" asked Zeke, echoing Cassie's thoughts.

"We have to free them," said Cassie. "Even the ones we weren't hired to find. And we better do it fast. Who knows when the kidnappers will come back."

"Agreed," said Zeke. "Robot, what is the most efficient method for returning all these animals to their homes?"

"Materialize all animals on board the space-ship, locate coordinates of homes, and send animals back. But first—remove this ridiculous costume from my body!" said the mechanical voice.

Cassie laughed nervously. Then she and Zeke helped Spot out of his penguin suit, and the three of them went to work. Fortunately, Spot had a large number of materializer disks in his supply compartment. They stacked the small animal cages—the ones containing birds or bugs or rodents—one on top of the other and sent the animals to the spaceship in groups of four or five. Then they moved to the larger cages.

"We should send these back one at a time," said Cassie.

"Why?" asked Zeke.

"Well, we can't stack a dog on top of a cat. It might try to reach into the cat's cage through the bars," said Cassie. "And to tell you the truth, I don't know too much about these other animals. Some of them might try to scratch at us or something. We better be careful."

"Okay," said Zeke, bending down and moving the next caged animal—a dog—into the center of the room so he would have enough space to throw the materializer disk.

Twenty minutes later the spies had almost reached the end of their task. Spot and Cassie were contemplating the now slumbering polar bear when Zeke called to them.

"Robot, assist me with this unpleasant-looking creature," he said. "It reaches out to claw at me whenever I get close to the cage."

Spot went to help Zeke. Out of curiosity Cassie followed and peered into the cage.

"What is it?" she asked. "It looks like a cross between a skunk and a weasel."

"It is an Earth animal from the family of mustelids called a wolverine," Spot reported. "The wolverine is an exceptionally strong animal for its size. It often attacks animals much larger than itself."

"Yikes!" said Cassie.

"I assume it would have no interest in a robot," said Zeke.

"That assumption would be logical," said Spot.

"Then *you* push the cage to the center of the room!" Zeke ordered.

At last only one animal remained. And it was going to be their biggest problem—literally. Although safely asleep, the polar bear weighed half a ton. Which meant that the spies couldn't push the cage. And the cage was backed up against the wall. Which meant that the materializer disk would not be able to complete its circling.

"I suppose we could let it out of the cage for a second and then throw the disk very quickly," said Zeke, staring at the sleeping bear.

"Are you crazy?" cried Cassie. "You look like an hors d'oeuvre to him!"

"What do you suggest?" asked Zeke.

Cassie stared at the cage. "I don't know," she admitted.

"There is a zepperk on board the spaceship," said Spot.

"A zepperk?"

"To zep the cage, of course," said Spot.

"Of course," said Cassie, rolling her eyes at Zeke.

"Go get it, Robot," Zeke ordered.

Zeke and Cassie waited in the tunnel while Spot returned to the ship. When the robot reappeared, he began complaining immediately.

"Those cages are all over the control room, and the animals are all making noises and . . . "

"Well, it's a good thing you don't have a sense of smell then," said Cassie.

"We are wasting time," said Zeke. "Robot, the zepperk!"

Spot handed Zeke a metal device that looked to Cassie like a devil's pitchfork. It was made of metal—all different colors of metal, with the green handle blending into the blue prongs, which gradually became purple, then red, and then orange at the tips.

Zeke handled the instrument expertly. He flipped a switch, and he bent his knees to better anchor his feet to the floor. Then, when the zepperk started vibrating wildly, he held the handle in both hands and raised the quivering instrument into the air. With some difficulty he managed to aim it directly at the polar bear's cage.

Two things happened at once. The cage moved, and the polar bear woke up. By the time Zeke had maneuvered the cage into the middle of the floor, the bear was a clawing, drooling, growling, very angry beast. And when the half-ton animal found he was not able to stand on his hind legs in the small cage, his roars became deafening. He rocked back and forth, back and forth in a furious motion until the cage tipped over on its side. A huge, hairy, clawed paw reached out through the bars toward Cassie and Zeke.

Cassie thought she was going to faint. "Do something!" she screamed at Zeke over the roars.

"What should I do?"

"I don't know. Let him out of his cage or something!' she shrieked. And then, "NO! I didn't mean that. I just meant . . . "

Now the bear's cage was rocking so violently that it began moving across the room. Cassie, Zeke, and Spot raced for a corner of the room, where they huddled together.

"What is wrong with him?" shouted Zeke.

"Perhaps it is the climate!" said Spot.

"What?

"The climate," Spot repeated. "According to all available literature, polar bears are accustomed to much colder weather. The temperature in this room is currently . . . "

"SHUT UP, SPOT!" Cassie screamed, her knees knocking together so hard she thought she could actually hear them over the roars of the bear. "Zeke—just send him back to the zoo!"

"Now?"

"Of course now!"

"But we do not have the coordinates!"

"Actually, I thought it might be necessary to return the large Earth creature directly to the zoo . . . ," said Spot. "I have brought the coordinates."

"Why didn't you say so!" Cassie yelled.

Zeke whipped a golden materializer disk from his pocket and punched in the coordinates as fast as the robot gave them to him. As the cage rocked closer and closer to the spies, the paw clawing furiously at the air, the roars so loud that Cassie had to cover her ears, Zeke threw the disk. It flew toward the polar bear and then began its rapid spiraling, sparkles trailing behind it. Then, suddenly, in a brilliant flash of light, the enraged polar bear disappeared from sight.

Cassie breathed a shaky sigh of relief.

"Whew," she said. "I'm glad that's over! Now let's get back to the ship."

Total confusion awaited them. The cages had materialized all over the control room, and not all of them had landed right side up. The noise from the complaining animals was deafening.

"Where is Spot?" asked Zeke.

"I don't know," said Cassie, thrilled to see that the cage that (stupidly) held the goldfish bowl had landed upright.

"Over here," droned a mechanical voice.

Cassie and Zeke raced to the corner where Spot's voice seemed to come from. They found him standing in the middle of a group of cages, struggling with the boa constrictor. The snake had wrapped itself several times around Spot's body, and its head was directly in front of Spot's face. The two of them were in the middle of a staring contest neither was going to win.

CHAPTER

"Whoa!" cried Cassie, skidding to a stop in front of the robot and grabbing at Zeke's arm. "Don't touch it!"

"Why not?" asked Zeke.

"Because the only reason that Spot is still alive is that he *isn't* living," said Cassie.

"I resent that!" said Spot. "I could be damaged beyond repair by this . . . this . . . creature's grip."

"Spot," said Cassie. "I don't know too much about boa constrictors—or about snakes at all. Look in your Earth biological systems banks and tell us how we can get this reptile off you without hurting ourselves. Meanwhile—Zeke, don't move."

The robot's computer whirred. "In order to communicate to a boa constrictor that you would like it to release its stranglehold," he said at last, "one should take hold of its head and stroke its body."

"I will do it!" said Zeke, reaching out toward the thick scales.

"NO, WAIT!" cried Cassie. "Then what, Spot?"

"Then the beast will release me," Spot stated.

"I mean, then what do we do with this snake slithering all over the ship?" asked Cassie. "We need to get it back in its cage."

"I believe we should simply send it back to Tyrell and let his brother deal with it," said Zeke.

"Oh yeah?" said Cassie, gesturing at all the nearby cages. "And how do you suppose we're going to do that without sending the rest of these animals with it? We'll have to get them out of the way first."

"An excellent point," said Spot, who hadn't moved an inch since the whole snake incident had begun. "Unfortunately, we do not have time."

"Why not?" asked Cassie.

"Because I believe the snake has increased its pressure on my body," said Spot.

"What does that mean?" asked Cassie.

The sound of creaking metal was her response.

"What are we going to do?" asked Cassie, trying not to panic. Seeing a clear spot in the middle of the room, she had an idea.

"Hey, Spot—what do boa constrictors eat?"

"Try the wolverine," suggested Spot.

"What?" said Cassie. "There's no way a snake is going to eat an animal that big."

"The wolverine will pick a fight with any creature," Spot reported. "Snakes and wolverines have been known to fight to the death."

"Really?" said Cassie. "Well, all right then." Cautiously she appoached the cage that held the vicious wolverine. The creature snarled, and Cassie felt a chill run up and down her spine. She took a deep breath and spoke.

"I'll move the cage into this space, Spot—close enough for the snake to see it. Then as soon as the snake goes for the wolverine, I'll pull the cage out of the way, and Zeke, you throw the materializer disk and send the constrictor home, okay?"

"Good idea!" said Zeke. "Wait a minute while I get the coordinates for Tyrell's house."

It took less than a minute for Zeke to locate the Hughes house in the ship's computer banks. Then he punched the numbers into a golden disk and returned to the robot's side. Cassie had not taken her eyes off the wolverine.

"Okay, Cassie," said Zeke. "Anytime you are ready."

Cassie did not carry the cage; she pushed it across the floor with her foot, stopping only when the wolverine was directly in the snake's line of vision. Then, eagerly, the spies waited.

But nothing happened.

Cassie nudged the cage a little closer.

Again nothing happened.

And then, suddenly, the wolverine made a horrid-sounding noise. And the snake hissed back. The wolverine tried to claw at the snake through the bars on its cage. The snake loosened its grip on Spot and slithered off his metal body. It moved so swiftly that Cassie didn't have time to slide the wolverine cage back.

"Cassie, the cage!" cried Zeke.

The snake was heading straight for the wolverine.

Cassie dove for the cage and pushed it out of the way.

Zeke threw the disk.

But Cassie was still too close.

"Cassie!" Zeke cried.

Cassie scrambled to get out of the way.

But it was too late. In a flash of sparkling light, the boa constrictor and Cassie vanished from the ship.

CHAPTER

7

The next sound Cassie heard was a boy screaming. She looked up from where she sat on the
floor and saw seven-year-old Tyrell Hughes pointing at her and yelling his head off. She didn't see
the snake anywhere.

"Hi, Tyrell," Cassie said, trying to sound as cas-
ual as possible.

The boy stopped screaming and looked confused.

"Wha-wha?" he stammered, trying to get the
words out.

Thundering footsteps brought a woman and a
large boy into Cassie's view.

"Tyrell?" said the woman, bending down at his
side.

"It's okay, Ma," said Tyrell. "This is Cassie."

"Why did you scream?"

"There was this lightning bolt, and then she
just appeared," said the boy. "It scared me. But
I'm okay now."

"Who are you? How did you get in here?" demanded the larger boy, moving into the room and looming over Cassie.

Cassie decided to ignore the second part of the question.

"Hi," she said, getting up and extending her hand pleasantly. "Cassie Williams, president of Spies, Incorporated at your service. We found your boa constrictor, and I'm here to return it."

The larger boy glanced around the room.

"Really?" he said suspiciously. "All I see is you."

"Well, to be perfectly honest," said Cassie, thinking quickly, "I kind of lost him at your front door, and . . ."

"SAMSON!" cried Tyrell at that moment.

Everyone looked to where Tyrell was pointing a chubby finger. The coiled tail of the snake stuck out from under a bed. Tyrell and his brother were so excited that they forgot all about Cassie and her strange entrance. But Mrs. Hughes never took her eyes off Cassie, and the spy was beginning to wonder how she was going to get out of the house and back to the ship.

"Well, I've got to go!" she said, trying to sound cheerful and businesslike as she headed for the door.

Mrs. Hughes blocked her path. "Just a minute, young lady. I have a few questions for you. For instance . . ."

At that moment the doorbell rang. Mrs. Hughes looked totally irritated when she realized that neither of her sons was about to leave the snake to answer it. Cassie followed her downstairs, hoping to slip out of the house as soon as possible.

It was Zeke.

"Hello," he said. "I am looking for my partner."

"Zeke!" cried Cassie, moving past Mrs. Hughes and out the front door.

"Wait a minute!" said Mrs. Hughes.

"Sorry. No time," said Cassie. "Got to run. Nice meeting you."

"But . . . "

"Run!" Cassie said to Zeke out the side of her mouth.

"Too suspicous," Zeke whispered back. "Speed walk!"

Cassie nodded, and the two spies broke into what was probably a record-settting speed walk. They didn't stop until they had reached the end of the block and turned the corner.

"Are you okay?" Zeke asked Cassie when they finally stopped to catch their breath.

Cassie nodded and laughed. "Whew!" she said. "That was a close one. Is Spot okay?"

"Robot is fine," said Zeke. "But there are still many animals remaining on the ship that should be returned to their owners."

Cassie glanced at the sky.

"Let's use a disk to get back," she said. "It will be getting dark soon, and I have to get home for dinner."

Cassie and the Spy from Outer Space materialized back on board the spaceship and spent the rest of the daylight hours returning animals to their rightful owners. Some of the pets they returned personally, handing them over to their delighted owners and collecting fees. Some they just sent back alone by disk. When the spaceship was finally empty of cages, Zeke gave Cassie one last disk so she could return home.

After dinner that night, Cassie watched the local news with her family. The lead story was about the mysterious reappearance of the missing polar bear. He had been found near the birdhouse, the reporter said. Zoo officials, hearing the roars of the bear, had rushed to tranquilize it and return it to its lair. Even stranger, reported the newsman, was the the discovery of a couple of rare birds, a baby spotted leopard, and a wolverine near where the bear had been found. All were in cages. All were unharmed.

But no one had any idea how the animals had gotten back to the zoo. Cassie was trying hard not to laugh when the phone rang.

"I'll get it!" she said, thankful for the excuse to

get out of the room before anyone noticed the huge grin on her face.

"Cassie Williams?" snarled a male voice on the other end.

"Yes?"

"Don't interfere with our mission again!"

"What?" said Cassie. "Who is this?"

"This is a warning. Stay away from the animals . . . *or you will regret it!*"

The next sound Cassie heard was a dial tone.

CHAPTER

Cassie slept fitfully all that night. The next morning she arrived at school early so she could talk to Zeke before classes started. When her alien friend showed up, she ran to greet him, babbling a mile a minute about the phone conversation. They agreed to meet after school to discuss what they should do.

But as the spies soon discovered, the phone call was only the first of their problems. As soon as they stepped inside the school, they were surrounded by screaming kids. Overnight most of the animals had been stolen again. Everyone wanted Spies, Incorporated to take their case.

All day long, students pestered Cassie about their pets. Neither she nor Zeke had a moment to themselves. Ben O'Brien was the worst of all. He couldn't believe Zeke and Cassie had left him behind the day before. He followed them everywhere, whining questions at them and getting in the way. He was driving Cassie crazy.

After school Ben insisted on following Cassie and Zeke to the house at the end of Whisper Wind Lane. The entire walk there, he continued his steady stream of questions and complaints.

"I can't believe you didn't wait for me yesterday. Are we three a team or what?" he said.

No one answered, but Ben didn't seem to notice.

"Are you sure that old spooky house is where you found the animals? How did you return them to everyone so fast? Did you have anything to do with that polar bear that appeared at the zoo yesterday? Why do you think they stole the animals again?"

Finally, even Zeke couldn't stand it anymore. He stopped walking and turned to face Ben.

"Spies are silent," he said simply.

"What?"

"He said spies are silent!" repeated Cassie, crossing her arms over her chest as she pierced Ben with one of her no-nonsense looks.

"Oh, really?" said Ben. "Since when?"

"Since now!" said Zeke firmly.

Ben shrugged and walked quietly for a while. But when the abandoned mansion at the end of the street loomed before them, he started talking again.

"So what made you go here in the first place? I mean—why does everything seem to start with this house?"

"Shhhh!" said Cassie. "Zeke, do you think we should proceed directly to the front door or hide behind the tree again?" she asked.

"How come you get to talk?" whined Ben.

"The tree," answered Zeke, ignoring him.

The three spies scurried to the large tree in front of the house and hid behind its massive trunk.

"Why are we hiding here?" asked Ben.

"Ben, what is wrong with you?" asked Zeke. "You have done nothing but complain since we left the school building."

"And you would have left me behind again if I didn't catch up with you," said Ben.

"Well, you're here now," said Cassie. "Do you want to help us spy or just be in the way?"

For a second Ben was silent, looking at his feet and kicking at the dirt beneath his shoes.

"Well?" said Cassie.

"Spy," muttered Ben.

"Fine," said Cassie.

"All clear," said Zeke. "Let us go!"

The three of them raced from behind the tree to the side of the old house and then around to the back, where Cassie peered in the small basement window while Zeke and Ben stood watch.

"There's someone moving around in there!" Cassie whispered.

"Really?" said Zeke. "Can you tell who it is?"

"Uh-uh," said Cassie. "It's too dark."

"Let me look," said Ben, dropping to the ground beside Cassie and squinting into the basement window.

"Yup. There's definitely someone in there," he said.

"Male," said Cassie.

"I'd say male," Ben agreed.

"Adult," said Cassie.

Ben agreed with that, too.

"And he's holding something," Cassie reported. "But I can't tell what it is."

"Cassie, use the night-vision periscope from your spy belt," said Zeke.

"I left it at home," said Cassie sheepishly.

"Hey, Zeke," said Ben. "Why don't you use those alien eyes of yours to see into this room?"

"He's not Superman!" Cassie snapped.

"I didn't say he was!"

"I do have superior vision," Zeke admitted, abandoning his lookout and dropping to the ground beside his friends. The three of them lay on their stomachs, peering through the window into the darkened basement.

Zeke gasped.

"That man is holding some sort of animal!" he reported.

"What's he doing?" asked Ben.

"He is just standing there," said Zeke, "as if he is waiting for someone."

"Well, we can wait, too!" said Cassie.

They didn't have long to wait. A moment later the door to the tunnel opened, and the man slipped inside.

"Should we follow him?" asked Ben.

"It could be very dangerous," said Zeke. "Especially after the threat Cassie received."

"Cassie got a threat? When?"

"I think we should go inside the house," said Cassie, scrambling to her feet.

Suddenly she screamed.

She was staring into what was absolutely the most hideous, deformed face she had ever seen. Huge, bulging red-veined eyes sunk into a fleshy, layered face.

It snarled at Cassie.

Cassie screamed again.

Zeke leaped to his feet. He saw the monster and gasped.

"Cassie, run!" he cried.

But Cassie's feet were glued to the ground.

The bulging eyeballs leaned in close to Cassie. She could smell the foul monster breath. Run, feet, run, she ordered. But now her knees were locked in place.

Suddenly, with a whoosh of air, the monster face toppled closer to Cassie, and the creature fell to the ground with a thud. Ben O'Brien leaped triumphantly off its back and cried, "RUN!" even as the hideous face was rising from the ground once more.

Cassie ran.

Ben ran.

Zeke ran.

They ran all the way to the other end of Whisper Wind Lane and all the way down the next street and the next. They did not stop until, gasping for air, they reached the safety of Cassie's garage.

CHAPTER 9

"Who—or what—was that?" Ben panted as he leaned against a wall.

"I don't know," Cassie gasped back. "But thanks for saving me!"

"From what?" asked Ben breathlessly.

"I don't know," Cassie said again. "But I sure wouldn't want to be hanging out with that—that—monster right now!"

"Was that an Earth species I am not familiar with?" asked Zeke, collapsing into a chair.

"NO!" shouted Ben and Cassie at the same time.

"Oh, there you are!" sang out a pleasant female voice. Cassie looked up and saw her mother standing in the garage doorway.

"You have a telephone call, Cassie," said Mrs. Williams.

"Okay, Mom," said Cassie.

A look of concern spread across Mrs. Williams's face. "Are you all right?" she asked her daughter. "You seem out of breath."

"We were having a race," said Cassie.

"Well, come inside and I'll make you all a snack."

Ben and Zeke followed Cassie into the house and sat at the kitchen table while she answered the phone.

"Cassie Williams?" rasped a male voice. Somehow Cassie thought she had heard the voice before, but she couldn't put her finger on where.

"This is Cassie."

"We told you to mind your own business or you would be sorry," threatened the voice. Now Cassie recognized who it was—the man who had called the other day.

"You don't scare me," said Cassie, lying.

"We can be very persuasive," said the voice. "And in case you need proof—have a nice day in school tomorrow."

Cassie joined her friends at the kitchen table and ate oatmeal cookies and milk and talked small talk with her mother. But the words "Have a nice day in school tomorrow" echoed over and over in her head. It sounded like a threat. But what did it mean?

Back in the garage, or Spies, Incorporated headquarters, Cassie told Ben and Zeke about the call.

Zeke thought for a minute. Then he seemed

to come to a decision. "I think we should give up the case of the missing animals," he announced.

"Why?" asked Cassie.

"For one thing, you are in danger, Cassie," said Zeke. "For another, we do not have any idea who that demon was or where he came from."

"Maybe we should let the police take care of this," said Ben.

Cassie couldn't believe it.

"What's the matter with you two?" she said. "Real spies get threatened all the time! We can't give up now."

"I heard you scream," said Ben. "You can't tell me you weren't scared."

"All I'm saying is that I don't think we should be scared off this easily. I mean, who else is going to solve this case if we don't?"

"The police," Ben suggested again. "We could go tell them everything that's happened up until now and let them take over."

"Oh great!" said Cassie. "I can't wait to hear what they have to say when we tell them how we used materializer disks to return the animals."

"Cassie has a good point," said Zeke. "We do not want the authorities to become suspicious of me. Perhaps we should continue to try to solve the case."

"Of course, you don't have to help us, Ben," said Cassie.

"Don't be ridiculous!" sputtered Ben. "I'm not afraid of some stupid monster and a threatening phone call or two."

"Neither am I," said Cassie.

"Neither am I," said Zeke.

But all three spies were lying. They were all afraid—though of what, they couldn't exactly say.

The next day in school Cassie learned just how persuasive the threatening phone caller could be. The trouble started at lunchtime when Marilee Tischler flounced over to the table where Cassie and Zeke sat eating.

"I want my cat back!" she announced in a huff.

"You got your cat back," said Cassie.

"As I already told Zeke, she is missing again," said Marilee.

"We know that, Marilee," said Zeke. "And we are doing our best to find her!"

"I'm not speaking to you at this moment, Zeke," Marilee said, smiling her sweetest smile at him. Her mouth turned into a snarl as she shifted her gaze back to Cassie.

"You can stop the act, Cassie," she said. "Everyone knows!"

"Knows what?" asked Cassie.

"Cassie Williams, I want my turtle back!" Toby Cranshaw plopped into a chair next to Cassie.

"When was your turtle stolen, Toby?" Cassie asked, surprised.

"As if you didn't know," snapped Toby. Cassie was shocked. Toby Cranshaw had always been a very nice, soft-spoken boy.

"Oh, Zeke," oozed Marilee. "Maybe you should find more honest friends. You are welcome to come sit with me."

"Marilee, what are you talking about?" asked Cassie.

Just then a fifth grader named Justin Cohen walked by the table, leaned in, and snarled, "Thief!" right in Cassie's face. Cassie was so stunned she couldn't think of anything to say. And when she could, all she could do was shout over the growing group of accusing voices. "Would someone *please* tell me what is going on!"

But the complaints just got louder, and no one told Cassie anything specific at all.

Things got worse as the day went on. Every class Cassie went to, every hallway she walked down was filled with kids staring at her and pointing and saying nasty things. But it wasn't until she was called to the principal's office at the end of the day that Cassie was able to find out what had happened.

"Cassie," Principal Levine said sternly, "there are rumors flying around this school that you have been stealing animals."

"What?" cried Cassie. "Why would I do that?"

"Why don't you tell me," said the principal.

"You aren't saying you believe the rumors, are you?" said Cassie incredulously.

"I am simply asking you if they are true or not," said Principal Levine.

"Of course they aren't true!" snapped Cassie. "The truth is that I found most of the animals that were stolen over the vacation. It isn't my fault they were stolen again, is it?"

When Cassie finally left the principal's office, she was in tears, uncertain as to whether she had been able to convince him of her innocence. She was so upset that she went straight home, not even stopping to see what Zeke was doing after school.

The Williamses' telephone rang nonstop the rest of the afternoon. By five o'clock, every single person had withdrawn their case from Spies, Incorporated. Cassie was sitting alone in the garage headquarters, her head in her hands, trying to figure out how she had gotten herself into this mess when suddenly a shadow crossed her path. She looked up, startled.

A man stood before her. He was dressed in a shapeless brown winter coat and had a brown felt hat pulled down to cover his eyes.

"We hope you've learned your lesson," snarled the man. "Now stay out of our way. Or next time we will tell the world about your friend Zeke!"

And with that, the man turned and left.

Cassie sat with her mouth hanging open. How

did he know about Zeke? Pulling herself together, she sprang into action. She grabbed her
spy belt and her jacket and followed the man. By
the time she got outside, she could see the
brown coat fading in the distance. She broke into
a run. But when she reached the end of the
street, the man was nowhere to be seen. It was as
if he had just disappeared into thin air.

CHAPTER

Cassie stood in the middle of the sidewalk, trying to figure out where the man had gone. She glanced up and down the street, puzzled.

Then, in the distance Cassie saw two people walking toward her. She held her breath and waited. But when the figures came into focus, she was disappointed. It was only Zeke and Ben. She waited until they had reached her side before blurting out, "Did you see a man?"

"What? No," said Ben.

"What man?" asked Zeke.

Cassie told them about the mysterious man in the brown coat.

"I recognized his voice," she explained. "He was definitely the same man who has been calling me. And Zeke, he knows who you are!"

"You were following him alone?" said Zeke, his voice full of concern.

"Sure. Why not?"

"You really should be more careful, Cassie."

"Zeke, did you hear what I said? That man knows who you are! He said he would tell everyone if we didn't stay out of his business."

Zeke thought for a moment.

"Perhaps he was just threatening," he said finally. "Perhaps he has no idea who I really am."

"Then why would he say he did?" asked Cassie.

"That is a good question," said Zeke. "And one that I intend to find the answer to."

"What are you going to do?"

"We're going back to the haunted house!" Ben announced.

"Really?" said Cassie, amazed.

"We have to get to the bottom of this, Cassie. There is too much at stake now," said Zeke. "The man said he knows my identity, and for all we know, he is also the person who started those rumors about you."

"Yeah," said Ben. "We asked all the kids at school where they had first heard that you took the animals, and no one could remember. Maybe that strange guy is behind it."

Zeke scanned the street and then pulled a golden pancake from his shoe.

"Ready?" he asked his friends.

"Ready," said Ben.

"Ready," said Cassie, grinning.

The three spies joined hands.

As her feet left the ground in a circle of twinkling light, Cassie's last thought was that she was lucky to have such great friends.

But no one was in the house at the end of Whisper Wind Lane. No one was in the basement. No one was in the tunnels. The people were gone, the animals were gone, the cages were gone. Even the smell of animals was gone.

There was nothing else for the spies to do. Confused and disappointed, they all went their separate ways.

The secret meeting was held on board the spaceship after school the next day. Present were Cassie Williams, founder and president of Spies, Incorporated; Zeke, cofounder and vice president; Ben O'Brien, manager; and Spot, honorary member. The reason for the meeting: to once and for all find the missing animals and get rid of whoever it was who was threatening the safety and happiness of the spies.

"Okay," said Cassie after calling the meeting to order. "Who's got any ideas?"

Her question was met with silence.

"Zeke?" said Cassie.

"I am thinking," said Zeke.

"Ben?"

"I'm thinkin', too," said Ben.

Cassie sighed. They were getting nowhere.

"I have an idea," said Spot.

"What is it, Robot?" Zeke asked.

"Lure the criminals with an animal," Spot stated.

"We already tried that," groaned Cassie.

"And may I remind you that you did not like being an Earth penguin at all," said Zeke, chuckling.

"A different animal," said Spot. "A rare animal."

"Hey!" said Cassie. "I think he's on to something. We could place an ad in the paper that says we're selling rare animals. Then when they call, we can arrange to meet them and follow them or something. . . ." Cassie let her thought trail off. It wasn't quite right yet.

"The criminals are too smart for that," said Zeke. "They would recognize your phone number, Cassie."

"Yeah, I know," said Cassie. "And every time we follow them, they seem to know."

"We have to catch them unawares," said Zeke.

"I've got it!" said Ben. "How about a post office box?"

Once again Cassie was astounded that Ben had a good idea.

"That's perfect, Ben!" she said. Ben beamed.

"What is a post office box?" asked Zeke.

"We place the ad," said Cassie, all excited. "And people have to answer by writing to a P.O. box number."

"Then we know who they are because they have to leave a return address or phone number," said Ben.

"What is a P.O. box?" asked Zeke, louder this time.

"And we'll use the money we made when we found the animals to pay for the ad and the P.O. box!" Cassie exclaimed.

"EXCUSE ME!" said Zeke.

Cassie explained to Zeke all about the United States postal system and what a post office box was. As she talked, Zeke began glancing over at Ben and looking more and more impressed. In the end even Spot had to admit it was a good idea.

"So, what kind of animal should it be?" asked Zeke.

"Let's not say," said Cassie. "There's a bigger chance that they'll answer the ad."

The spies left the spaceship and divided up. Ben ran over to the post office before it closed and rented a P.O. box. Cassie and Zeke went to the offices of the *Hillsdale News*.

The next day, in the advertising section of the paper, in a small box near the bottom, their ad appeared:

FOR SALE: Rare Animals.
Interested parties leave phone number.

Now all they had to do was wait for someone to answer.

CHAPTER

11

The next afternoon the spies went to the post office and checked their box. But there was nothing in it that day—or the next.

Meanwhile, more and more animals were missing. Cassie started dreading school. So many of her classmates were now convinced that she had something to do with the kidnappings that she could hardly walk down the halls without hearing nasty comments or being glared at in obvious ways. Marilee Tischler was making the most of Cassie's misfortune, and Cassie vowed to get even with her someday.

Ben was the big surprise. For as long as Cassie had known him, he had been the bully of her class, and all the kids were scared of him. Now he was using that power to protect Cassie. More than once she heard him threaten to beat someone up if they didn't stop teasing her.

The days moved by slowly for the spies. Zeke gave Ben karate lessons in the afternoon on board the spaceship while Cassie did her homework. She had lost her appetite for spying—at least until they solved this case. *If* they ever solved it.

And then one day two letters appeared in the post office box.

"Two?" said Ben, bouncing on one of the cushiony clouds of light in the spaceship. "What do we do now?"

"Stop bouncing, Ben!" said Cassie, handing him a glass of a green Triminican liquid that tasted like melted Jell-O.

Ben stopped bouncing and took the drink.

"Well? What *do* we do?" he repeated.

Cassie shrugged and carried a glass across the room to where Zeke sat.

"I think we should answer both letters," said Zeke. He took a glass off the tray and smiled his thanks at Cassie.

"I do, too," Cassie agreed. She settled onto a cloud and took a sip of her drink. "Did they both leave phone numbers?"

Zeke glanced at the letters in his hand and nodded.

"I don't suppose Spot has rigged up a telephone on this ship yet?" Ben asked hopefully.

"No," said Zeke. "Do you think he should?"

"Of course he should!" said Cassie. "But for this, a pay phone is better, anyway. First, though, we need a script!"

"And a plan!" Ben added.

This was what they came up with:

The Plan

1. Write a script telling the criminal (monster?) where to go to purchase the rare animals.
2. Use a pay phone so the call cannot be traced.
3. Let Ben read the script because he is the best one at disguising his voice.
4. Hide, and when the criminal (monster?) shows up, make sure it's him, and then follow him back to wherever the animals are hidden.

When they were finished, Cassie read the plan out loud from her notebook.

"Well? What do you think?" she asked.

"There is a detail missing," said Zeke. "Where is the appointed meeting place?"

"That's part of writing the script," said Cassie. She flipped to a new sheet of paper in her notebook and chewed on her pencil for a minute. Then she wrote the following:

SCRIPT: "Hello. Thank you for answering our ad for rare animals. If you would like to discuss the possibility of purchasing these animals, be at the post office at four P.M. today. A person will approach you and ask, "Do you like animals?" You will respond, "I like the rare ones best."

Cassie looked up from her notebook, pleased with herself, and read the script aloud to Ben and Zeke.

"The post office?" said Ben. "I don't think so."

"Why not?" asked Cassie.

"Where are we going to hide?"

It was a good point. The Hillsdale Post Office was squeezed between the Hillsdale Diner and the Hillsdale Beauty Salon and was located on a heavily trafficked street.

"Well, where then?" asked Cassie.

"What about the school yard?" Zeke suggested.

Cassie shook her head. "No. That's too much of a giveaway that we're kids."

"I've got it!" cried Ben. "The zoo!"

"Why the zoo?" asked Cassie.

"For one thing, it's really crowded," said Ben.

"Not only that," added Zeke. "The criminal will take our offer more seriously if he thinks we actually have access to rare animals. An excellent idea, Ben!"

Ben looked so proud Cassie thought he was going to explode.

"Okay!" she said. "The zoo it is!"

"One more thing," said Zeke. "I think you

should arrange the meeting for four P.M. tomorrow. We do not want to appear too eager."

Cassie groaned. All this waiting to fix her reputation was driving her crazy. But Zeke was right. She fixed the script to say tomorrow at the zoo. Then the three spies went in search of a pay phone to set their plan in motion.

CHAPTER 12

At exactly ten of four, the president, vice president, and manager of Spies, Incorporated hid themselves across from the entrance to the Hillsdale Zoo and waited. They weren't hidden so much as disguised—two little old men and a little old lady sitting peacefully on a bench, waiting for a bus.

"So how are we going to know when he shows up?" asked Cassie, straightening her mother's bifocals on her nose.

"He's a monster, remember?" said Ben.

"Yeah, maybe—but you talked to two people, Ben," Cassie reminded him.

"I told one of them to show up at four thirty," said Ben.

"You did?" said Cassie. "That was smart. I didn't hear you do that."

"Well, I did!" said Ben, offended. "And one of them will be a monster, so it shouldn't be too hard to tell."

75

"The two of you are being ridiculous," said Zeke. "Obviously the monster is not going to show up. And if he does, he will be disguised."

"Oh, yeah," said Cassie.

Ben grumbled, "Oh, yeah," too.

At two minutes after four, the spies noticed a strange-looking man in a trench coat lurking outside the entrance to the zoo. They watched him for five full minutes. He kept consulting his watch and looking up and down the street.

"That's him all right!" said Cassie. "Okay, Zeke. It's up to you. We'll be listening."

Zeke checked to make sure the microphone was in place inside his coat. Then Cassie activated the listening device, and Zeke crossed the street and approached the man. Ben and Cassie held their breath and listened.

Zeke was using his best little old man voice. It was terrible.

"Do you like animals?" he asked the man.

"I like the rare ones best," said the man, answering in the code Ben had told him to use.

"Which rare one is your favorite?" asked Zeke.

"Oh. I like only rare bugs," said the man.

Cassie and Ben looked at each other. That was a very strange answer. They had fully expected the man to be interested in all rare animals.

"Do you like kangaroos?" asked Zeke.

"No. Bugs," said the man firmly.

"Maybe he already has a kangaroo," Ben whispered to Cassie.

"Are you kidding?" said Cassie. "Where would he get a kangaroo? Something is wrong."

"Do you like koalas?" asked Zeke, who had never seen one but was reciting from memory the list of animals Cassie had come up with to test the man.

"No marsupials," said the man. "Bugs."

"Well, what about a Komodo dragon?" asked Zeke.

"BUGS!" said the man loudly.

"Forget it!" Cassie said to Ben. "This definitely isn't our criminal. There's absolutely no way he already has a Komodo dragon. Signal Zeke."

Ben rose from the bench and crossed the street slowly, tugging at his beard. He looked more like a kid in his grandfather's clothes than an old man, but no one seemed to notice. As he passed Zeke, he tipped his hat, signaling him to give up. Then he proceeded down the street as planned.

Zeke informed the man that he had no bugs, and the man left in a huff. Then the three spies met up again at the bench. The first man had not been their criminal. But they weren't too disappointed, because they were positive the second one would be.

At four thirty a boy about fourteen years old arrived at the entrance to the zoo. By a quarter to five, he was still the only person lingering at the appointed place.

"Maybe they sent a kid," said Cassie hopefully.

"Yeah, right!" said Ben.

"Well, try it anyway," said Cassie. "It's our last hope."

The kid was just a kid who collected rare snakes. By five o'clock the spies were back on the bench, silent and upset. Their plan had not worked.

"Some spies we are!" said Cassie.

"What are we going to do now?" asked Ben.

No one had any ideas. In the end they decided that Ben would cancel the post office box the next day. Then they would meet at Cassie's house and try to figure out what to do. Right now they all just wanted to go home and forget about it.

CHAPTER 13

The next afternoon Ben practically flew through the doorway to Spies, Incorporated.

"Ben, calm down!" said Cassie grumpily. It had been a horrible day in school, and she was in a terrible mood. Zeke didn't even look up from the book he was reading.

"LOOK!" shouted Ben at the top of his lungs.

Cassie and Zeke looked. Ben was waving a letter in his hands.

"What is it?" asked Cassie, a tiny little bit of excitement creeping into her voice.

"I went to cancel the post office box and they made me check it one last time and this was in it. Wait until you hear it!" said Ben.

Ben read the letter.

"Interested in ALL RARE ANIMALS. Will pay ANY PRICE. Leave list of animals and prices in P.O. Box two-three-six-six-eight-one."

"That's him!" cried Cassie. "I can feel it!"

"That's what I thought!" Ben cried back.

The three spies sat grinning at each other for a full minute. Then Cassie leaped from her seat to get a sheet of paper so they could write a response.

"What should we say?" she asked.

"Use really, really rare animals," said Zeke.

"And make the prices outrageous so he'll think we're serious," said Ben.

"Oh no," said Zeke suddenly.

Zeke sounded so alarmed that Cassie looked up from the list she had started to make.

"What is it?" she asked.

"Think about it, Cassie," said Zeke. "Why no phone number? He is going to watch us put the response in his post office box. He is going to hide and follow us they same way we were going to hide and follow him."

"Wow!" said Cassie. "Who is this guy?"

"I do not know," said Zeke. "But we must be very, very careful."

The spies *were* very careful. They spent a long, long time creating the response, deciding that a simple list with no other words on the page was best. Then they typed the list out on Cassie's father's computer so whoever read the letter would not be suspicious of fifth-grade handwriting.

Komodo Dragon	$27,000.00
Poison Arrow Frogs	$400.00 each
Tarantula	$900.00
Snow Leopard	$20,000.00

The following day was Saturday, which meant the post office was open only until noon. No one watching the entrance that morning would have seen anything unusual—just a rather strange-looking dog, sniffing around the fire hydrant on the sidewalk in front. When the postwoman showed up to open the office, the dog ran inside playfully. The postwoman laughed and tried to shoo the dog away, but the dog ran back inside, and the woman laughed again and left him alone.

At ten after nine the dog trotted back out of the post office, sniffed around the hydrant once more, and ran off down the street. No one paid any attention as it pushed its way into some bushes in the small park at the end of the street.

"You were perfect!" Cassie whispered to the dog.

"I especially liked the hydrant sniffing!" Ben added.

"That was humiliating!" said Spot, yanking at one of the curly wigs that covered his body.

"Robot, leave that wig on!" Zeke ordered.

"But . . . "

"You must remain disguised until we are back on board the ship."

"Here we go!" said Cassie, peering through the binoculars from her Super Deluxe Spy Kit.

Zeke, Ben, and Spot crouched at Cassie's side and watched the man walking through the post office doors.

"Are you sure it's him?" Ben whispered.

"Absolutely," said Cassie. "That's definitely the man who threatened me in the garage. Same brown coat and everything."

The man in the brown coat came out of the post office a moment later. He was holding an envelope in his hand. He looked up and down the street suspiciously and then walked swiftly around the corner. The spies sprang into action, following the man but keeping a good distance. They were fast and clever, dodging behind trees and bushes a split second before the man turned to check behind him. The spies followed the man to the edge of town, where much to their surprise he suddenly headed into the field where Zeke's spaceship was parked.

"You don't think he found the ship?" Cassie asked breathlessly when the three spies and Spot slowed down to see which way the man would go.

As if in answer to her question, the man veered away from Zeke's ship, and the spies followed him to a completely different part of the field. When the man finally stopped and looked around him once more, the group of four plunged to their stomachs in the tall, dewy grass.

That was where they were when to their amazement the man pulled a small device from his pocket and activated it. A moment later another spaceship came into view.

CHAPTER 14

A staircase descended from the ship. The man climbed up it and disappeared into the ship only seconds before the whole thing became invisible again.

No one said anything for a very long time. And then they all started talking at once.

"Another ship!" said Zeke.

"What kind of ship was it?" asked Cassie.

"Where did it come from?" asked Ben.

"Who is that man?" asked Cassie.

"Where . . ."

"Who . . ."

"NOBODY MOVE!" Zeke ordered loudly.

Everyone quieted down.

"They could be watching through the window of the ship to see if anyone is in the field," Zeke explained. "Everyone stay where they are."

Everyone obeyed.

"Robot," said Zeke, "report on the ship."

"I did not see enough of it," said Spot. "Vines

of some variety have been hung over much of the space vehicle's body to disguise it when the invisibility shield is not activated."

"Then we will have to wait," said Zeke.

They remained lying down in the field and waited. And waited. And waited.

"What are we waiting for?" Ben finally whispered.

"I don't know," Cassie whispered back.

"We are waiting for some sign of life to appear," said Zeke.

"What kind of life do we think is aboard that ship?" asked Cassie.

"I think we are going to have an answer very soon," said Zeke. "Look!"

The interior of the ship was becoming visible through a slowly opening doorway.

The three spies and the robot watched as the panel slid open and the staircase slowly descended again. When a creature appeared at the top of the staircase, all three spies gasped at once. It was the hideous-faced monster they had seen at the house at the end of Whisper Wind Lane.

"Robot, identify species!" Zeke ordered.

Spot was silent for a moment.

"ROBOT!"

"I am unable to identify this species as being from anywhere in our galaxy," reported Spot.

"What?" said Zeke. "Well, what galaxy is it from?"

Spot was silent again, searching his computer banks for the information Zeke requested. Finally, he answered.

"I find no life-form that matches this description in my computer banks."

The creature turned and disappeared back inside the ship.

"Robot, return to our ship and program all necessary information into the main computer banks. And scan this spaceship if possible. We must find out who these beings are!"

The robot scurried off through the high grasses in the direction of the Triminican spaceship while the spies remained behind and kept watching. They didn't have to wait long. The monster with the hideous face reappeared at the top of the stairs.

Cassie's heart was pounding a mile a minute as she watched the horrid creature climb down the staircase and into the field. A moment later another creature appeared, and then another.

"They look identical!" she whispered, disgusted and terrified.

"Perhaps we should return to the ship," Zeke whispered back.

"Too late!" snarled a voice behind them.

In one motion all three spies jumped to their feet and found themselves staring into the bulging eyeballs and fleshy skin they had seen once before.

Cassie screamed and ran.

Zeke screamed and ran.

Ben screamed . . .

When Cassie turned around in midrun, she saw the most awful thing. The creature was climbing up the staircase of the ship. And he was dragging a kicking, screaming Ben with him.

A moment later the ship became invisible again.

Cassie collapsed in the field. When Zeke reached her, he threw himself down in the grass beside her.

"Where's Ben?" he gasped.

"He's . . . he's . . . " Cassie couldn't get the words out. Her eyes blazing with fear, she raised her arm and pointed in the direction of the ship.

"NO!" cried Zeke. "They got him?"

Cassie nodded.

"They . . . got . . . him," she gasped. She felt like she was going to cry.

Cassie and Zeke used a materializer disk to return to Zeke's spaceship. The moment they arrived on board, Zeke raced to the robot's side.

"Report!"

"I have identified the life-forms," said Spot.

"Well?"

"They are disguised. I am having difficulty identifying the nature of their disguises."

"Forget about their disguises," Zeke demanded. "Who are they?"

"They are Delphs!"

Cassie gasped. "DELPHS!" she cried. "What are we going to do?"

"Cassie, try to calm down," said Zeke.

Just then a loud beeping sounded from a section of the control panel at the far end of the room.

"What's that?" asked Cassie.

Zeke turned to Cassie, his eyes wide. "We are being hailed," he said.

"By whom?" asked Cassie, even though she already knew the answer.

"Robot, respond to the message but do not speak," said Zeke.

"What does that mean?" Cassie whispered.

"We will beep them back," said Zeke.

"Accomplished," said the robot.

"Now open a channel to receive the Delphs' message," said Zeke.

Spot punched at the control panel. A moment later Cassie heard a high-pitched whine and then a voice—a familiar voice—one that she had heard more than once on the telephone.

"If you want the Earth boy, bring us the rare animals! Midnight. Tonight. Or he will become another one of our specimens!"

And then, suddenly, all communication stopped.

"They have shut off contact," reported Spot.

Cassie groaned. "Those idiots actually think we have rare animals!"

"The Delphs are quite serious about experimenting on their specimens," Spot reminded the spies.

"Yeah, I remember," said Cassie, shivering as she recalled her experiences in Zeke's galaxy. "Zeke, what are we going to do?"

"We are going to locate a rare animal, of course," said Zeke.

"Where?" asked Cassie.

"Not me again!" said Spot.

"No, of course not," said Zeke. "This time we need a real rare animal."

"The zoo?" asked Cassie.

"Not rare enough!" said Zeke. "Tell me, Cassie. Where would we find a real Komodo dragon?"

15

Spot read off the computer screen.

"The Komodo dragon is a member of the monitor lizard family. Growing up to ten feet long, the Komodo dragon is the largest lizard on planet Earth. It scavenges on dead animals and catches deer, pigs, and wild boar. Komodo dragons live on the island of Komodo and other islands east of Java.

"Java!" said Zeke. "Great. Cassie, where is this Java?"

Cassie shrugged her shoulders.

"I have absolutely no idea," she said.

"Spot?" Zeke asked the robot.

"Checking," said Spot. A moment later he resumed reading from the computer screen.

"Java is the largest of the fourteen thousand islands that make up the country of Indonesia."

"Fourteen thousand islands!" said Cassie. "WOW!"

"Most impressive," Zeke agreed. "We do not have islands on Triminica."

"The capital of Java . . . ," Spot continued.

"Enough, Spot," said Zeke. He turned his attention to Cassie. "Do you think we should go to this Java and capture a Komodo dragon?"

Cassie shook her head slowly.

"It might take an awfully long time to find one," she said. "And besides—how do we know the Delphs will really trade Ben for a rare animal? How do we know this isn't all a trap? Maybe they'll just capture us the minute we show up."

Zeke nodded as he listened.

"You are absolutely correct, Cassie," he said. "Perhaps we need more information before proceeding. Robot, are you able to identify how many Delphs are on board that ship?"

From his position at the computer's control panel, Spot programmed in the question. A moment later, he responded.

"There are four Delph life-forms on board the ship, one human life-form, twelve reptile life-forms . . . "

"Okay, okay," said Cassie laughing nervously.

"Only four!" said Zeke hopefully. "Maybe we can overpower them and get Ben back without a rare animal."

"Will you leave the other creatures in the hands of the Delphs?" asked Spot.

"Spot!" exclaimed Cassie, delighted in spite of

her fear. "Are you adding compassion to your list of emotions?"

"Simulated emotions," Zeke corrected her.

"Whatever," said Cassie.

"I am merely recalling the agitation of the gorilla at the zoo and the other animals in the tunnels," said Spot. "They did not seem to relish being caged, and I cannot imagine that they would like to be experimented on any more than you would."

"He's right, of course," Cassie said to Zeke. "We have to return the animals to their owners."

"And we need to get rid of the Delphs once and for all!" Zeke added.

"So," said Cassie, ticking off each item on a finger. "We have to get Ben back, return the animals, and get rid of the Delphs." She grinned at Zeke mischievously. "A typical day for any spy at the Interstellar Spy Academy, right?"

"I have an idea!" said Spot. "What about those horrible snakes?"

"You mean the boa constrictor that tried to strangle you?" asked Cassie.

"Affirmative," said Spot.

"What about the snakes?" asked Zeke.

"*We* could not overpower the Delphs," said the robot. "But a hundred snakes could certainly back them into a corner."

"A hundred snakes!" exclaimed Zeke, laughing. "Does anyone have any other ideas?"

95

But Cassie wasn't laughing.

"Zeke, every pet store in town carries snakes, and there's a snake house at the zoo. We could borrow them, couldn't we? Maybe not a hundred, but enough to scare the Delphs."

"But the snakes are not rare!" said Zeke.

"We can tell the Delphs we're sending over a Komodo dragon," said Cassie.

"And then what?" asked Zeke.

For the next hour Cassie, Zeke, and Spot huddled together, plotting and planning. By the time Cassie had to return home for dinner, they were ready. They knew where they were going to get the snakes, how they would outsmart the Delphs, and how to return the animals. They even figured out what to do with the Delphs. Nothing could go wrong. Or could it?

CHAPTER

16

The first thing that went wrong was that Cassie overslept. She accidentally set her alarm for eleven A.M. instead of P.M. She awoke with a start at five of midnight and threw the materializer disk without even brushing her teeth.

But when she materialized on board the spaceship, there was no Zeke, no Spot, and no snakes.

Suddenly the hailing frequency crackled with static, and a voice boomed, "Answer, Triminican!"

Cassie stood frozen to the floor, staring at the control panel, uncertain of what to do.

"ANSWER, TRIMINICAN!" the voice commanded.

In a cloud of twinkling light, Zeke materialized beside Cassie. She breathed a sigh of relief and felt her feet again.

The hailing frequency whined, and the voice, this time filled with fury screeched, "TRIMINICAN, RESPOND!"

Zeke winked at Cassie and moved toward the control panel.

"We have your Komodo dragon. Prepare to receive," he answered.

"Negative, Triminican. You will materialize in the field outside the ship, and we will allow you to board."

"Understood," said Zeke. "Over and out."

"Oh no!" said Cassie after Zeke had ended contact. "What are we going to do? And Zeke, where are the snakes?"

"Calm down," said Zeke. "Let me explain. We realized that there was no way the Delphs—who are very suspicious, as you know—would let us just send something over. So we came up with a slightly different plan."

"I don't understand," said Cassie. "Where's Spot?"

"At the zoo."

Zeke pulled a device from his pocket. Cassie recognized it immediately. It was one of the walkie-talkies from her Super Deluxe Spy Kit. Spot had souped them up so they had a very powerful range.

"Robot, come in!" Zeke said into the walkie-talkie.

"Ready and waiting!" said Spot's voice, loud and clear.

"I will return," Zeke said to Cassie, and raced out of the room. He reappeared a moment later with a solid metal cage. The tiny airholes were too small to see inside.

"What's in there?" asked Cassie.

"Nothing," said Zeke, and grinned.

Cassie grinned, too. She was beginning to understand.

"Just one last detail to take care of," said Zeke, moving toward the control panel. He hailed the Delph ship.

"What?" snarled a voice on the other end.

"The Komodo is quite vicious," said Zeke. "We suggest you have at least four of your people present to handle it."

"Let us worry about that," snapped the voice. "Are you ready?"

"We are ready."

The two spies materialized in the field only a few feet from the other spaceship. Almost immediately the other ship became visible and the staircase descended.

Cassie squeezed Zeke's hand. Zeke squeezed back. Then the two spies went to save their friend.

Slowly they mounted the stairs to the ship. When they reached the top and stepped into the drab, dimly lit control room, the staircase closed behind them with alarming speed.

Suddenly the monstrous-looking creatures appeared. Three of them—advancing on Zeke and Cassie. Cassie tried to stop herself from being so frightened. She knew they were Delphs in disguise, and that this was the plan. But she hated being backed into a corner. And now one of the creatures was reaching out, reaching toward Zeke. . . . The Delph yanked at the metal container and, when he had it, backed away.

Cassie let out her breath.

"And the boy?" asked Zeke.

One of the creatures, the only one holding a weapon, motioned with the laser gun for Cassie and Zeke to walk ahead of him. They had no other choice—they were here to save Ben. But as they walked down a set of narrow, winding stairs, Cassie saw Zeke pull the walkie-talkie from his pocket and whisper into it.

"Now, Robot!"

Suddenly there was a roar of anger from above them. "We have been tricked!"

The Delphs had opened the cage that was supposed to contain the Komodo dragon.

There was another roar from above, but this one was of fear, not anger. And it was followed by more roars and shrieks of panic and orders being issued and things being thrown. Zeke looked at Cassie and grinned. The Delph behind them looked confused for a moment, as if he did not know what to do.

"Zeke," Cassie whispered. "Let's run!"

There was only one way to go. The two spies

raced down the stairs. But as they reached the corridor below, Cassie felt the heat from a laser blast aimed at the floor near her and screeched to a halt. Zeke came to a full stop beside her. Cassie felt her hair being yanked roughly as a voice snarled into her ear.

"Do that again and I will put you in with the bear!"

The two spies were forced toward a room at the end of the hall. As they stepped through the doorway, Cassie thought she was going to be sick. The smell was intense. But it wasn't only the smell—it was the sight. Every single missing animal was there. Some were chained to the wall, but most were caged. And in a corner of the room, in a cage of his own, was Ben O'Brien.

Cassie gasped and grabbed Zeke's arm. But Ben, all sluggish and drugged looking, barely even looked at them.

The Delph called out in his own language, and the fourth Delph appeared from an adjoining room. This Delph was also in a monster mask, and he was carrying a set of keys. He moved swiftly to the same cage that Ben was in, unlocked it, and motioned for the two spies to enter.

Cassie looked at Zeke in desperation. Zeke shrugged and tilted his head toward the cage. Reluctantly Cassie moved toward it.

And that was when Zeke tripped her. As Cassie

flew through the air, she could hardly believe what had happened. She fell hard against the Delph with the weapon, and the two of them crashed to the floor.

"Cassie, roll!" yelled Zeke as he rammed his body full force into the other Delph—the one with the keys—knocking him to the ground and landing a karate chop to his neck.

Cassie obeyed instantly, rolling off the Delph and watching as Ben sprang to life, lunging for the Delph and expertly disarming him.

"Now move!" Ben snarled at the astonished creature.

Cassie's mouth dropped open.

"Cassie, help me!" Zeke ordered from where he knelt over the unconscious Delph. Cassie moved quickly to her friend's side and helped him drag the Delph into the cage. Then the three spies tied up both the Delphs and locked them in the cage. When they were done, Cassie threw her arms around Ben.

"Ben, that was great!"

Ben squirmed but looked proud.

"How did you do that? How did you get the weapon away from him?" Cassie asked, letting him go at last.

Ben grinned. "It was that new karate move Zeke taught me the other day," he said.

Zeke laughed.

"What's so funny?" demanded Ben.

"To be honest," said Zeke, "what I taught you was a fighting technique used by the Delphs."

Ben chuckled.

"They are Delphs, you know," he said. "With Halloween masks on."

"We know," said Zeke.

"But Ben, you looked drugged," said Cassie. "What happened?"

"Actually, Zeke taught me how to do that, too," Ben explained. "I wanted them to think I was completely out of it."

"You were quite good at it," said Zeke. "I was not completely certain that you would be able to assist."

"Well, you were both great!" Cassie said, grinning and linking her arms through the arms of her two friends.

"Don't relax so quickly, Cassie," said Ben. "There are two more of them upstairs."

"Zeke's got them trapped by a bunch of snakes," said Cassie.

"Really?" said Ben.

"We should go check," said Zeke. "Ben, help me bring up one of those big empty cages—and the keys."

"What are we going to do with them?" asked Ben as they hurried down the corridor toward the staircase that led up to the main room of the ship.

"We've got that all worked out," said Cassie,

following her friends up the stairs. She was about to explain further, but as she entered the control room of the ship, what she saw left her absolutely speechless. The two remaining Delphs were clinging to pipes on the ceiling. Below them four alligators were looking up and licking their lips.

"Zeke!" cried Cassie, backing away as fast as she could. "Those aren't snakes!"

"Spot informed me that they were members of the reptile family," said Zeke. "We found them much more menacing than snakes."

"So do the Delphs," said Ben, laughing.

"If you want us to call them off, throw down your masks!" Zeke ordered the Delphs.

The masks were swiftly ripped off and thrown on the floor, where an angry alligator ripped them to shreds.

"TRILL!" said Cassie from where she cowered behind Ben.

Trill was the evil Delph leader who had been responsible for kidnapping Cassie and Ben after taking over the Triminican ship on its journey home.

"I just have one question," Zeke called up. "Did you follow us back here for some reason or return simply to collect animals for your barbaric experiments?"

"What do you think?" spat Trill.

"I think," said Zeke firmly, "that you can stay up there for the rest of your life for all I care."

Zeke took the walkie-talkie from his pocket and contacted Spot.

"I am ready for the coordinates, Robot," he said.

Spot gave Zeke the coordinates he needed, and Zeke punched them into a golden disk that he removed from his shoe.

"Ben, I will throw this disk and return the alligators," he said, loudly enough so the Delphs could hear him. "But first help me slide this cage out for our friends here. As soon as the alligators are out of the way, the Delphs will climb down and get into it peaceably. If they do not, Spot will materialize the alligators straight back. Right, Robot?"

"Affirmative," said Spot's voice through the walkie-talkie.

Ben, thrilled with his new position of responsibility, gave the cage a good push toward the center of the room. Zeke threw the disk and Cassie watched in amazement as the owl creatures scurried along the pipes on the ceiling and down the walls like some sort of rodents. Practically cowering, they got into the cage. Ben rushed forward and quickly turned the key in the lock.

"It worked!" he shouted.

"Just wait," growled Trill from the cage. "Just wait till next time."

"There will be no next time," said Zeke briskly. Then, he spoke into the walkie-talkie: "Spot, we are ready for you."

Spot materialized on board the Delph ship and went immediately to the ship's control panel.

"Just as I suspected," reported Spot. "They have a sophisticated materializer beam that is operated from here."

"What does that mean?" asked Cassie.

"It means that the Delphs stole the animals by finding and programming coordinates for each creature and then materializing them on board the ship from here, does it not, Spot?" said Zeke.

"Affirmative," said the robot.

"So that's how they got all those animals out of the tunnels so fast!" said Cassie.

Zeke nodded. "I guess they must have still been building the cages on the ship and they needed a place to hide the animals," he said.

"Or else they couldn't stand the smell!" said Ben chuckling.

"Robot, can we return the animals the same way?" asked Zeke.

The robot punched a few buttons on the control panel.

"Affirmative," he said. "The coordinates for any animal that materialized on board this ship are still logged in the computer banks."

"Exactly how do we operate this materializer beam?" asked Cassie.

"There must be a chamber somewhere," said Spot.

Zeke located a cylindrical chamber just off the main room and called Spot over to look at it. The robot agreed that it was where the animals must be placed.

"Well, let's get started," said Cassie.

It took three spies and one robot almost three hours to return all the pets to their rightful owners and all the wild animals to their natural environments.

As the sun began to rise slowly in the sky, only one more chore was left to be done.

"It is unfortunate that we cannot send the Delphs back to their planet with this device," said Zeke, motioning at the Plexiglas chamber.

"Where will we send them?" asked Ben. "Like your ship, theirs can't break out of our galaxy for six more months until the planets are correctly aligned."

"That is true," said Zeke, grinning at Cassie. "But it does not mean we cannot send them somewhere in this galaxy."

"What?" said Ben. "I don't understand."

"You explain, Cassie," said Zeke. "It was your idea."

"Well, you know how I love to read all those

books on the planets?" said Cassie eagerly.

"Uh, sure," said Ben.

"Well, the planet Neptune has a moon scientists say certain species could live on."

"Species such as the Delphs," said Spot.

"You're kidding!" Ben exclaimed.

"It's not going to be comfortable living on it or anything," said Cassie. "But we won't hurt the Delphs, and they won't be on Earth to hurt any more animals or threaten Zeke."

"So we're going to send them there and then destroy their ship?" asked Ben.

Cassie shook her head.

"No. We'll send them in their ship. But Spot has drained out any excess fuel from their fuel banks so they won't be able to go anywhere else. They'll have the ship to live inside—they just won't be able to use it to go anywhere."

"Well? What do you think?" Zeke asked Ben.

"It's great!" Ben exclaimed.

"Are we ready, Spot?" asked Zeke.

"Affirmative!" reported the robot. He had just completed programming the ship's computer to take the Delphs to the remote moon they would soon be calling home.

"Let's have a ceremony," said Cassie. "I want to see their faces when they find out where they're going."

Downstairs the three spies faced the Delphs in their cages. It was no surprise to any of them that the two Delphs that had been tied up had already managed to get out of their restraining ropes. It was just a matter of time before they were all out of their cages. But by then it would be too late. Spot had locked in the coordinates to the moon, and not even a clever Delph would be able to alter the course of the ship.

"Trill and you other Delphs," Cassie said ceremoniously. "For mean and nasty crimes against poor defenseless animals, and for kidnapping Ben and threatening Zeke, you have been sentenced to spend the rest of your days alone. Completely alone. You will live on a moon that circles a planet in our solar system. It is so far away that no Earth person has ever been to it. Good-bye and good riddance!"

Zeke and Ben cheered Cassie's speech.

The Delphs roared in anger. As the three friends left the room, they could hear the threats and insults being hurled after them.

Back on the bridge of the ship, Spot activated the computer. Then he and the spies all held hands and materialized to a place far away in the field.

Two minutes later, they watched as the ship launched. It seemed to crack open the dawning sky, leaving a blazing trail of fire behind it as it carried the Delphs far, far from Earth. As it disappeared from sight, Cassie yawned.

"It's time for bed," she said. "Brunch at my house when we wake up?"

"Is your dad making pancakes?" asked Ben.

"Always on Sundays," said Cassie. "Except when it's French toast.

"So I guess things will be back to normal in school on Monday," said Cassie. "Thanks." She smiled at her friends.

"Another great adventure," said Zeke.

"Definitely," Ben agreed.

Zeke handed out materializer disks, and then, in a twinkle, he and Spot were gone. Cassie watched Ben disappear, too, before throwing her own disk. Then she stood for a minute, alone, staring at the sky, where long ago she had stared and only dreamed of creatures from outer space and of friends to spy with. It had been another great adventure, indeed.

About the Author

Debra Hess has done a fair amount of spying in her life, and is pretty sure that a few of her friends are from outer space. The author of several popular books for young readers, she lives in Brooklyn, New York, with her husband, their daughter, a lot of fish, and two newts.